Jake's Best Thumb

Ilene Cooper   ILLUSTRATED BY Claudio Muñoz

DUTTON CHILDREN'S BOOKS

*For all the thumb (and finger) suckers. And with thanks to Dale Matten
and the kindergarten students at Lincolnwood Elementary School.*
—I.C.

To Orlando, thumbs and all, welcome!
—C. M.

DUTTON CHILDREN'S BOOKS
A division of Penguin Young Readers Group
Published by the Penguin Group
Penguin Group (USA) Inc., 375 Hudson Street, New York, New York 10014, U.S.A.
Penguin Group (Canada), 90 Eglinton Avenue East, Suite 700, Toronto, Ontario, Canada M4P 2Y3 (a division of Pearson Penguin Canada Inc.)
Penguin Books Ltd, 80 Strand, London WC2R 0RL, England
Penguin Ireland, 25 St Stephen's Green, Dublin 2, Ireland (a division of Penguin Books Ltd)
Penguin Group (Australia), 250 Camberwell Road, Camberwell, Victoria 3124, Australia (a division of Pearson Australia Group Pty Ltd)
Penguin Books India Pvt Ltd, 11 Community Centre, Panchsheel Park, New Delhi - 110 017, India
Penguin Group (NZ), 67 Apollo Drive, Rosedale, North Shore 0632, New Zealand (a division of Pearson New Zealand Ltd)
Penguin Books (South Africa) (Pty) Ltd, 24 Sturdee Avenue, Rosebank, Johannesburg 2196, South Africa
Penguin Books Ltd, Registered Offices: 80 Strand, London WC2R 0RL, England

Published in the United States by Dutton Children's Books,
a division of Penguin Young Readers Group
345 Hudson Street, New York, New York 10014
www.penguin.com/youngreaders

Designed by Irene Vandervoort

Manufactured in China   First Edition

ISBN: 978-0-525-47788-4

10 9 8 7 6 5 4 3 2 1

Like most people, Jake has two thumbs.

His right thumb is smooth and pink and joins the rest of his fingers when they're tucked in a mitten or wrapped around a crayon.

His left thumb is wrinkled and spends much of its time in Jake's mouth.

Jake likes his left thumb best.

When it came to doing things with one thumb occupied, Jake was a master.

Watching TV, walking his dog, Rex, and drawing pictures were all easy to do with his thumb in his mouth.

Getting dressed and riding his bicycle were a little harder.
But usually Jake managed.

Most of the family did not approve of Jake's best thumb.
His mother said, "Jake, you're going to ruin your teeth. They will start to stick out. You could wind up looking like a rabbit."
Jake examined his teeth. They seemed fine. As for looking like a rabbit, well, that might be interesting!

His sister said, "Jake, quit now or you might still be sucking your thumb when you grow up. You can't be a doctor or a dentist with your thumb in your mouth."

Who cares? thought Jake. *I can be a fireman or a lion tamer. I can climb a mountain or fly to the moon.*

His father said, "Jake, only little kids suck their thumbs. You're a big kid."

Jake frowned. *Really?* He stood back to back with his sister. She was much bigger. The rubber tree in their living room was bigger. Even Rex was bigger.

Jake's grandmother, her brow creased with worry, asked, "My darling, when will you stop sucking your thumb?"

Jake thought about it. When he was sad, his thumb made him feel happy. When he was scared, his thumb made him feel brave. When he was tired, he put his best thumb in his mouth and fell asleep right away. He especially needed his thumb at night.

Jake climbed onto his grandmother's lap and leaned against her. "Not for a while."

"That's what I thought," Grandma said with a sigh.

Only Uncle Matt seemed to understand how much Jake needed his thumb.

"How's that thumb of yours?" he asked when he came for a visit.

"Everyone wants me to stop sucking it," Jake answered.

"Oh, what do they know?" Uncle Matt made a face. "Is it still in good shape?"

Jake looked at it. "I think so."

Uncle Matt examined Jake's thumb.

"In the pink, I'd say. Just the right number of wrinkles—gives it some character. Strong. Bold. A prince among thumbs."

"Thank you," Jake said.

"And you were wise to latch on to your thumb instead of a Teddy bear or some other stuffed animal. Know why?"

Jake shook his head.

"Because you can't lose it." Uncle Matt roared with laughter. "It's attached."

When spring came around, Jake had to remove his thumb from his mouth to blow out the candles on his birthday cake.

During the summer, he needed both hands when he carried the rings down the aisle at his cousin's wedding.

In the fall, Jake started kindergarten. There, he needed his best thumb more than ever. The school was huge, swarming with noisy kids. Honest-to-goodness big kids. Even the other kindergartners seemed bigger than him, especially a boy named Cliff.

Mrs. Matten was Jake's teacher. She had a friendly face and wore her hair in a ponytail. After the parents left, Mrs. Matten asked her new students to sit in a circle on the floor, but Jake didn't hear her because he was busy looking around the large, bright room. It was filled with toys and books and plants and posters. Being in school was exciting, and a little bit scary. Jake popped his thumb into his mouth.

Cliff pointed at Jake. "Look," he bellowed, "a thumb sucker!"

It took Jake a minute to realize Cliff was talking about him.

The other kids knew right away. "Thumb sucker." The whispers went around the room.

Mrs. Matten clapped her hands. "Eyes on me, please."

Jake looked at Mrs. Matten, but he could feel that most of the eyes in the classroom were still on him. He sat down and folded his hands, but his thumb, wiggling back and forth, was too tempting. Very soon it was comfortably back in his mouth.

"Thumb sucker," Cliff hissed.

Later, as the children were lining up for recess, Mrs. Matten leaned over and whispered in Jake's ear, "What do you think about trying not to suck your thumb in school? Is that a good idea?"

Jake thought it was a good idea. And he did try. Sometimes he stuck his best thumb in his pocket.

Sometimes he even stuck it in his ear.

But sometimes it was in his mouth before he noticed it was there. Whenever that happened, it seemed like Cliff was always nearby.

"Thumb sucker."

Jake hated being called a thumb sucker.

But he still liked sucking his thumb.

One day Jake was lying down on his mat during rest time. A girl named Nell was next to him. She had thick black curls and curious brown eyes.

"What are you thinking about?" Nell asked Jake.

"My thumb."

"You wish it was in your mouth, don't you?"

Jake pulled his thumb out of his pocket. "Yes." He looked at Nell. "Do you . . . ?"

Nell shook her head.

"Oh." Jake started to turn away.

"But I don't like to go anywhere without Kitty Harold."

"Kitty Harold?"

"My little stuffed cat. He's in my cubby right now." Nell looked longingly over at the shelf where the children kept their things. "I take him everywhere. I can't fall asleep at night without him."

Jake nodded. "Everybody needs something at night."

The next day at recess, Jake and Nell were playing pirates. Instead of sucking his thumb, Jake was pretending it was a sword. He pointed it at Nell menacingly. "You must walk the plank, Lady Nell."

"Oh no, I won't!" Nell declared. She brandished her own thumb. "I have a sword, too."

Cliff was on the monkey bars, watching them. He started laughing at Jake and Nell.

"Dumb, dumb, having a sword fight with your thumbs," Cliff said in a singsongy voice.

"Bet you can't do this!" he yelled. He did a somersault over the bar and hung by his knees. As he dangled there, something fluttered out of his pocket and fell to the ground. Cliff didn't notice, but Jake and Nell did.

Nell ran over, picked it up, and handed it to Jake.

It was an old piece of blue material about the size of a hankie.
Faded and fuzzy, it looked like a rag. Jake was about to throw it
away when he ran his finger over the worn satin ribbon around
one of the edges. Suddenly, he knew just what the scrap was.

Nell looked at Jake. She had guessed, too.

"A piece of blankie," Jake whispered.

Nell nodded. "My brother had one just like it."

Pops of power bubbled inside Jake. Suddenly, he felt big.
"Hey, Cliff," Jake called loudly. "I think you dropped
something. It fell out of your pocket."

That got Cliff's attention. He dropped off the monkey

bars, stuck his hand in his pocket, and urgently started poking around. Then he jammed his hand in the other pocket. Nervously, he looked at Jake.

Jake danced in front of Cliff, holding the piece of blanket.

"Give it back!" Cliff said, lunging toward him.

But Jake was too quick. "No way. It's all mine, you . . . you . . .
Blankie Rub-ber!"

"What did you call me?" a shocked Cliff asked.

"A Blankie Rub-ber. This is a piece of your baby blanket, and you keep it in your pocket so you can rub it all day." Jake could tell by the look on Cliff's face he was right. "Blankie Rub-ber!" he yelled triumphantly.

Nell chimed in, "You were teasing Jake about sucking his thumb, and the whole time you needed your blankie."

Cliff stood still. He didn't look so big now. He looked like he might cry. "Can I have it back?" he asked, holding out his hand.

"Why should I give it to you?"

Cliff looked down at his shoes. "Because I need it. I can't fall asleep without it."

Jake and Nell glanced at each other. They both knew what that was like.

Clutching Cliff's blanket in his hand had made Jake feel big. But now, seeing how upset Cliff was, it made him feel awful.

Keeping his fingers lightly curled around the scrap, Jake said,
"If I give it back, do you promise you won't call me thumb sucker
anymore?"

"I promise," Cliff answered hopefully.

"How do I know you'll keep your promise?"

"Because if I don't, you'll call me a blankie rub-ber," Cliff said
with a lopsided grin.

Jake had to smile, too, as he handed over the piece of blue
blanket. He was surprised he felt even bigger when the blankie
was back in Cliff's pocket.

That night, in each of their houses, Cliff, Nell, and Jake brushed their teeth, said their prayers, and got into bed. Cliff was holding his blanket. Nell was cuddling her kitty. Jake was sucking his thumb.

Tomorrow, Cliff thought, *I'll leave my blankie at home.*

Tomorrow, Nell thought, *Kitty Harold will wait on my bed until I get home from school.*

Tomorrow, Jake thought, I won't suck my best thumb all day.

But everybody needs something at night.